SYLVESTER & TWEETY

READ THE MYSTERY

The Jewel Robbery

Bath · New York · Singapore · Hong Kong · Cologne · Delhi · Melbourne

Story by Sid Jacobson
Pencils by Pablo Zamboni and Walter Carzon
Inks by Duendes del Sur
Color by Barry Grossman

First published by Parragon in 2008
Parragon
Queen Street House
4 Queen Street
Bath BA1 1HE, UK

PARR 8204

ISBN 978-1-4075-2632-4

Printed in USA

The Posh Society Ball was one of the biggest events of the year and Granny wanted both Tweety and Sylvester to look their very best for the party.

"It's the sixth time she's bathed me today," Tweety muttered. "Pwetty soon I'll have no feathers at all."

Sylvester and Tweety looked handsome standing with
Granny at the entrance of the Posh Society Ball. Inside
the ballroom, the richest people in town were all there to
celebrate the event. The evening was guaranteed to be
more exciting than Granny imagined.

They strolled into the huge ballroom.

"Look at the jewels in this place," Sylvester whispered.

"Yeah," Tweety answered in a low voice. "And they're all so pwetty, too." And all worth a lot of money!

Granny was invited to the party because her grandfather, Percival Posh, was the society's founder. His portait hung near the entrance to the ballroom.

"That's Grandpa Percy," she said to her pets as they passed it. "He was once the richest man in town, but lost every penny by the time I was born."

PERCIVAL POSH
FOUNDER OF OUR SOCIETY

The group's president, Warren Van Cash, greeted Granny. But soon, he was distracted by all the guests showing off their pricey jewels to one another and left the room.

"Look at my million dollar bracelet," said one.

"And my three million dollar ring," said another.

Granny smiled, but said nothing about her simple, five dollar ring.

As the band began to play and people started dancing, guests continued to come up to Granny to describe their jewelry.

Tweety whispered to Sylvester, "I think I've heard about fifty million dollars of jewelwy alweady."

And that's when it happened!

"I've been robbed," Mrs. Moolah exclaimed. "My million dollar necklace is gone!"

"And so is mine!" "And mine!" "And mine, too!"

These cries echoed throughout the ballroom. Soon, everyone was in an uproar.

"This is a perfect time to catch that stupid canary," Sylvester thought, smiling to himself. "With all their troubles, who's going to pay attention to me?"

Tweety noticed Sylvester's look and immediately dashed away through the crowd.

Sylvester knocked over a platter of food, spilled two bowls of lemonade, broke the bass drum of the orchestra and jumped on to all eighty-eight keys of the piano in his pursuit of the fleeing Tweety.

Tweety ran through people's legs, under tables, and over empty chairs. But Sylvester didn't give up the chase. People were so concerned with the big robbery, they didn't even notice him.

Granny also missed seeing Sylvester's mischief. She was busy comforting her friends who had lost great fortunes in the robberies. "Someone please call the police!" she finally called out, and twenty people quickly rushed to their cell phones.

But Tweety wasn't thinking much about the robbery.
He had to make sure he stayed away from the cat's claws.
He hid among the lights of the gigantic chandelier hanging
high over the ballroom.

From this view, Tweety saw a heavy woman in a lavish blue gown walking past the huge portrait of Granny's grandfather, Percival Posh. She poked her hand behind the portrait.

"Whatever is that woman doing?" Tweety asked himself.

Tweety kept his eyes on the woman. She walked back and forth, going from a bejeweled woman on the ballroom floor to the portrait of Granny's grandfather. Then she'd start all over again. Each time this happened, someone would call out that she had been robbed.

"Could she be the wobber?" Tweety asked. The canary
then wondered how he could possibly stop her and still
keep himself safe from Sylvester.

"But I've got to do something," he decided. And he did!

Tweety quickly flew down from the chandelier and moved toward Percival Posh's portrait. Spotting him, Sylvester's eyes lit up and he headed for Tweety.

"I'm going to get you!" he exclaimed, as he ran toward the portrait.

"I hope I know what I'm doing," thought Tweety.

The woman in the blue dress once again walked toward the portrait. Tweety flew by and landed squarely on the picture frame. Sylvester leaped toward Tweety and the portrait.
"Oh, no!" the woman cried, in a deep, loud voice.

CRASH! SLAM! BANG!

"Look!" screamed a huge group of people.

Sylvester had missed Tweety, but crashed into the portrait, slamming it against the wall and unloosening a treasure trove of jewelry that had been hidden behind it.

The woman in the blue dress was Warren Van Cash, the group's president. He had dressed up as a woman to commit the robberies.

"I'd lost everything," he blurted, "and I had to get it back."

"Percival Posh lost everything, too," said Granny, "but he always remained decent and honest. And the proud founder of this society!"

"You two really solved the mystery," said Granny, kissing
Tweety and patting Sylvester. "You're quite a good team
when you work together."
"Oh, brother," Tweety muttered. "That will never happen!"